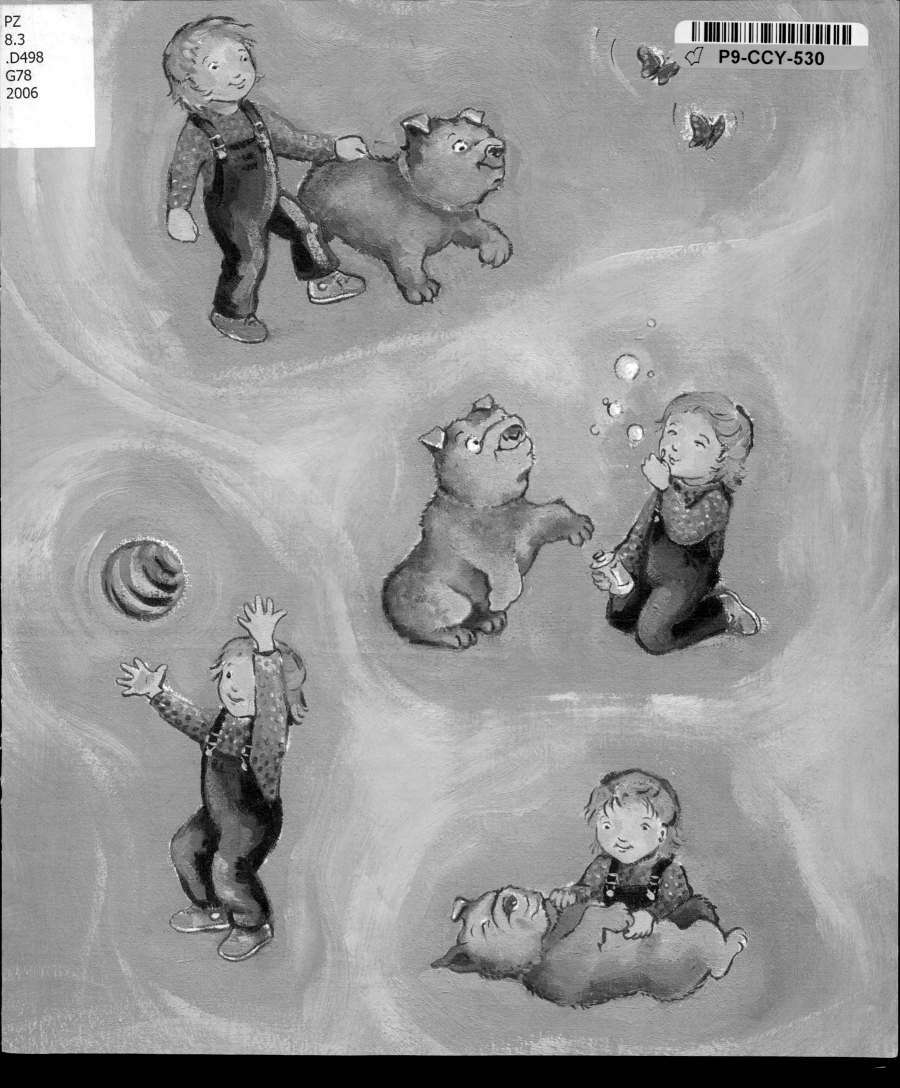

To my mother,
Winifred Bruce Luhrmann,
with love.

# Grumpy Gloria

by
ANNA
DEWDNEY

VIKING

Gloria was glum and grumpy.
Out of sorts.
Sad and lumpy.

A brand-new doll? It's time to pout!
Gloria felt so left out.

Gloria, what can we do?
Would you like a doggie chew?

Sullen, scowly, sulky, slumpy . . .
Gloria was staying grumpy.

Maybe we should brush her hair!
Little dog hairs everywhere.

Snort and snuffle, squint and scowl.
Gloria was feeling foul.

What's the matter with the dog?
Maybe she would like a jog!

Trotting,

 panting,

 wheezy,

  dumpy . . .

Jogging made the dog **more** grumpy.

Maybe Gloria feels dirty—
get the sponge and soap and squirty!

Steamy, scrubby, slimy, soapy . . .
Gloria was mad and mopey.

Maybe she would like a toy!
Which of these would she enjoy?

Squeaky? Squawky? Jumpy? Jabby?
Gloria was feeling crabby.

Maybe she would like a game!
Dress in costume! Choose a name!

Pirate maiden, frilly-frumpy?
Gloria was **really** grumpy.

Hey, I know! She wants a ride!
Put the doggie up inside.

Weave and wobble,

scream and shout.

Grumpy Gloria—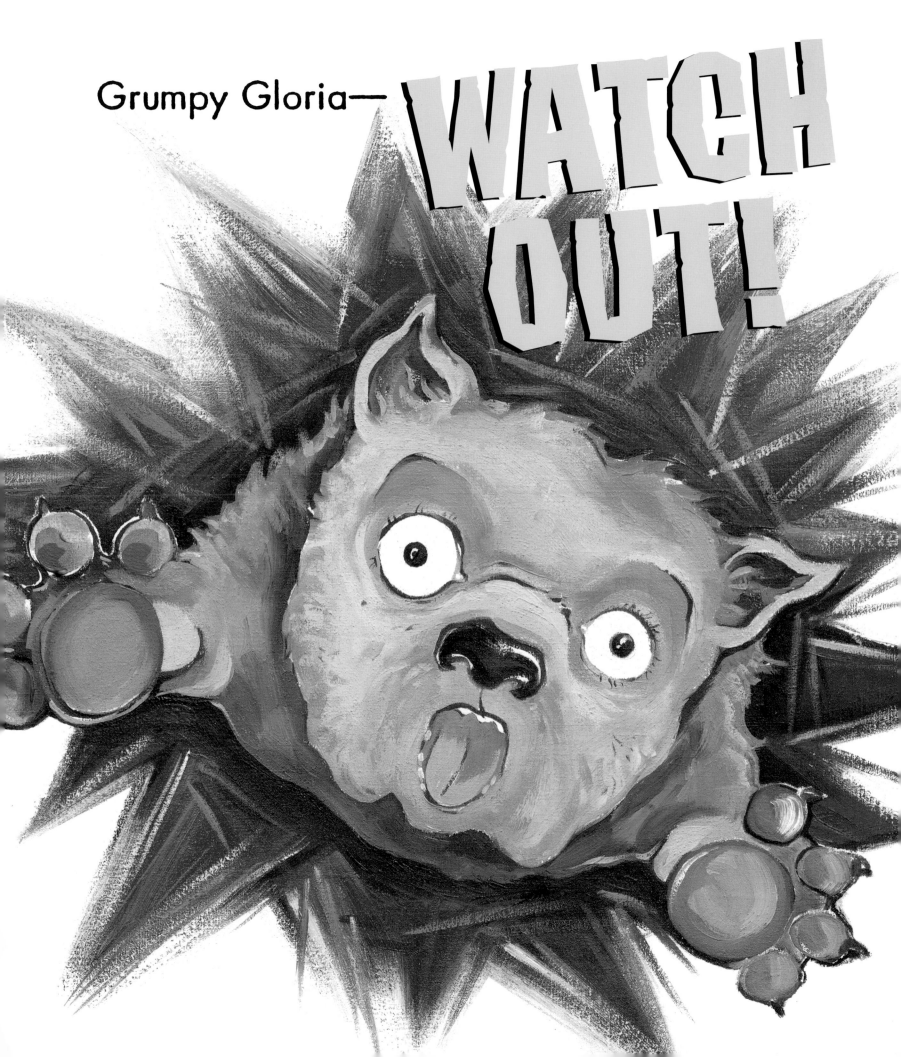

# WATCH OUT!

Grumpy, slumpy, gritty, grouchy.
Dirty, dusty, blinky, ouchy . . .

Wiggle-waggle.
Look! Guess who?

Gloria, there's
room for two!

Grumpy Gloria, we are done.
We're sorry you're not having fun.

But Gloria—unlike before—
wasn't grumpy . . .

. . . anymore.

VIKING
Published by Penguin Group
Penguin Young Readers Group, 345 Hudson Street,
New York, New York 10014, U.S.A.
Penguin Group (Canada), 90 Eglinton Avenue East, Suite 700, Toronto,
Ontario, Canada M4P 2Y3 (a division of Pearson Penguin Canada Inc.)
Penguin Books Ltd, 80 Strand, London WC2R 0RL, England
Penguin Ireland, 25 St Stephen's Green, Dublin 2, Ireland (a division of Penguin Books Ltd)
Penguin Group (Australia), 250 Camberwell Road, Camberwell,
Victoria 3124, Australia (a division of Pearson Australia Group Pty Ltd)
Penguin Books India Pvt Ltd, 11 Community Centre, Panchsheel Park, New Delhi – 110 017, India
Penguin Group (NZ), Cnr Airborne and Rosedale Roads, Albany, Auckland 1310,
New Zealand (a division of Pearson New Zealand Ltd)
Penguin Books (South Africa) (Pty) Ltd, 24 Sturdee Avenue, Rosebank, Johannesburg 2196, South Africa

Penguin Books Ltd, Registered Offices: 80 Strand, London WC2R 0RL, England

First published in 2006 by Viking, a division of Penguin Young Readers Group

1 3 5 7 9 10 8 6 4 2

LIBRARY OF CONGRESS CATALOGING-IN-PUBLICATION DATA
Dewdney, Anna.
Grumpy Gloria / Anna Dewdney.
p. cm.
Summary: Family members try various ways to cheer up their grouchy bulldog.
ISBN 0-670-06123-9
[1. Bulldog—Fiction. 2. Dogs—Fiction. 3. Stories in rhyme.] I. Title.
PZ8.3.D498 Gr 2006
[E]—dc22
2005033646

Manufactured in China
Set in Kennerly
Book design by Kelley McIntyre